MEN IN BLACK
Official Agents' Handbook

WARNING!
UNAUTHORIZED
USERS WILL BE NEURALYZED!

You'll conform to the identity we give you.
You will have no identifying marks of
any kind.
You will not stand out in any way.
Your entire image is crafted to leave no
lasting memory.
You're a rumor, recognizable only as
déjà vu.
You don't exist; you were never born.
Anonymity is your name.
Silence is your native tongue.
You are no longer part of the system.
We're above the system.
Over it. Beyond it.

We are the Men in Black.

MEN IN BLACK™

OFFICIAL AGENTS' HANDBOOK

WRITTEN BY
DAWN MARGOLIS

NEWMARKET PRESS
NEW YORK

This book published simultaneously in the United States of America and in Canada.

97 98 99   10 9 8 7 6 5 4 3 2

Library of Congress Cataloguing-in-Publication Data

Margolis, Dawn
   Men in black : official agents' handbook / written by Dawn Margolis.
      p. cm.
   ISBN 1-55704-345-0
   1. Men in black (Motion picture)   I. Title.
PN1997.M4353.M37 1997
791.43'72—dc21   97-29687
                                               CIP

Quantity Purchases

Companies, professional groups, clubs, and other organizations may qualify for special terms when ordering quantities of this title. For information, write Special Sales, Newmarket Press, 18 East 48th Street, New York, NY 10017, or call (212) 832-3575.

Designed by Mercedes Everett

Manufactured in the United States of America

"Men in Black
Is an Equal Opportunity Employer"

Dear New Recruit:

Congratulations. You have been chosen to join the most important law enforcement team on Earth. For more than thirty years, the Men in Black (MIB) have monitored alien activity on Earth, provided intergalactic immigration services, and represented the planet Earth in fifth-dimension foreign affairs.

Your job is to investigate any and all unlawful acts committed by aliens.

In addition to the laws specifically outlined in this Manual (see Alien Penal Code, page 12), space creatures are expected to abide by all the same laws as U.S. citizens—except jaywalking. (Our feeling is, cross at your own risk.) See to it that these laws are strictly observed.

The use of physical force against aliens should be considered a last resort.

Intergalactic law mandates that nonviolent negotiation tactics be employed before forcibly subduing a space criminal. But, in the end, we expect you to use whatever means are necessary to keep the planet safe.

It is also imperative that all MIB investigations remain a secret. In 1967 the United Intergalactic Community (UIC) unanimously decided that because humans are "too stupid for their own good" it is advisable to keep alien activity confidential.

Your role as an MIB agent should not be taken lightly. The safety of the planet rests in your hands. Every man, woman, child—not to mention cat and dog—depends on you. There can be no life, liberty, and pursuit of happiness without the Men in Black.

That is all. Good luck, and Godspeed.

Sincerely,

May

May
Director of Human Resources

IDENTITY RELEASE FORM FOR NEW AGENTS

I _____, being of
(state your name)

sound mind and body, do hereby irrevocably terminate all rights to my current identity. I understand that all personal documents—including birth certificate, driver's license, and social security number—will be expunged from the record. I also agree to have my fingerprints extinguished. I recognize that this procedure may be painful, but that once commenced it cannot be aborted. This document supersedes and revokes all prior claims to said identity.

This declaration is made on this _____
date

day of _____, 19 _____
month   year

_____
Declarant

_____ residing at _____
witness   address

MIB
NOTARY

Kate Kradaby

Field Placement Evaluation

The following survey will help us determine where you would best serve the MIB. Complete this form using a number two pencil.

Choose the best answer for the following questions.

1. If spacecraft A is traveling due west at 30 times the speed of light, and spacecraft B is traveling due east at 40 times the speed of light, at what point will the two spacecrafts collide?
   a. when the moon is in the seventh house.
   b. when Jupiter aligns with Mars.
   c. when peace will guide the planet, and love will rule the stars.
   d. never, because spacecraft A's flight was canceled.

2. I am _____ with zero gravity.
   a. very comfortable
   b. somewhat comfortable
   c. not at all comfortable

3. I _____ travel(ing) at speeds in excess of 5 million miles an hour.
   a. enjoy
   b. don't mind
   c. would rather be stuck in traffic for 6 hours than

4. Which of the following adverse conditions sounds least appealing?
   a. being trapped on a planet where surface temperatures exceed 300 degrees.

b. being sucked into the belly of a sea-sick space alien.

c. being swindled by a many-tentacled alien of indeterminate nationality.

5. **Do you have a family history of any of the following (circle where applicable):**
   a. schizophrenia   b. pyromania
   c. paganophobia   d. kleptomania
   e. hemophilia   f. xenophobia

6. **Do you see a glass as**
   a. half empty   b. half full
   c. a window into another dimension

7. **If approached by a two-toed sloopery snitch, you would**
   a. invite him in for coffee.
   b. blow his brains to Kingdom Come.
   c. ask him what happened to his other eight toes.

8. **Which of the following factors prompted you to join the MIB?**
   a. The chance to fight for truth, justice, and the American way.
   b. A moral obligation to safeguard the citizens of planet Earth.
   c. The generous 401K plan.
   d. Alternate option was death by firing squad.

9. **On a scale from 1 to 10 rate your experience level using each of the following weapons.**
   a. bow and arrow   _____
   b. shotgun   _____
   c. revolver   _____
   d. light saber   _____
   e. atomic warhead   _____
   f. vaporizing cannon   _____
   g. proton torpedo launcher   _____
   h. retractable ion laser   _____

10. Do you have allergies to any of the following?
    a. asteroid dust   b. animal dander
    c. moon cheese (Muenster excluded)
    d. braised tofu

11. Do you have a fear of:
    a. heights   b. small spaces
    c. flying   d. alien abductions

12. Which came first the chicken or the egg?
    a. the chicken   b. the egg
    c. I'm still trying to figure out whether the egg came before the eggplant.

13. You're the spacecraft driver. At your first stop, five mergatroids get on. At your next stop, one mergatroid gets off, and four cephlapoids get on. On the Lesser Moon of Luppa Lou, four bipodic crustaceans get on, and one cephlapoid gets off. At Alpha Centauri, two Oomish Kanish get on and clone themselves. If the toll to cross the Golden Gate bridge is $1 per passenger, how much will it cost you?
    a. $16   b. $25
    c. Nothing, because you'll never get a spacecraft across the bridge in all that traffic.

14. Have you ever done any jail time?
    Yes   No
    (If so, please include a letter of recommendation from your warden.)

15. Do have formal training in any of the following areas?

    a. computer programming
    b. electrical engineering
    c. teleportation

    d. space aeronautics
    e. psychic healing
    f. fire walking

16. Do you have a history of psychotic episodes, sleeping fits, or cannibalism?
Yes   No
(If no, explain why not in the space provided below.)

_____

17. Do you believe in:
    a. Big Foot
    b. The Loch Ness Monster
    c. Santa Claus
    d. The Tooth Fairy

18. Please rank in order of preference your favorite TV shows.
    a. bowling   _____
    b. infomercials   _____
    c. soap operas   _____
    d. sitcoms   _____

19. Have you ever worked for a division of the company before? If yes, please list department and dates of service and the reason for your departure.

_____
_____
_____

20. How would you like the MIB to dispose of your remains?
    a. Freeze my body until such time as scientists can figure out a way to bring me back to life.
    b. Sprinkle my ashes over a tranquil forest.
    c. Leave me to rot in a wooden box six feet under.

Alien Penal Codes

The following laws apply to aliens during their stay on planet Earth. A copy of these laws shall be disseminated to all intergalactic visitors upon arrival.

Alien Ordinance # 371.43.E (Exposure) Aliens are not to disclose their true identity. An alien who reveals or threatens to reveal him/her/itself may have his/her/its visa immediately revoked. Furthermore, the alien can be fined up to two million space rooples.

Alien Ordinance # 900.34.B (Parking) A full-size spacecraft may not be parked in a compact spacecraft parking space. Violators will be ticketed and towed.

Alien Ordinance # 8675.30.M (Trespassing)
Aliens found wandering outside their designated zone area shall be considered absent without leave. If found, said alien shall be immediately deported.

Alien Ordinance # 383.38.M (Psionic Powers)
The use of telekinesis, mental telepathy, clairvoyance, and levitation is strictly prohibited. Violators will be placed in a locked room and forced to listen to Barry Manilow songs continuously for a period of up to 24 hours.

Alien Ordinance # 777.56.P (Curfew) No alien shall be present in public spaces between the hours of 2 a.m. and 5 a.m. unless said alien has received prior authorization from the office of Time, Space, and Dimension. Failure to comply will result in immediate deportation.

Alien Ordinance # 3483.21.O (Abductions)
Abducting a human for alien observation is strictly prohibited. Any alien caught in the act of beaming a human up to the mother ship for organ extraction, alien inhabitation, or general observation shall be banished to a black hole for eternity plus 10 years.

Alien Ordinance # 641.54.E (Skimming)

No alien shall depart the planet without first clearing takeoff with outbound immigration. Unauthorized departures will result in the revocation of the pilot's intergalactic flyer's license.

Alien Ordinance # 201.937.D (Sock Snatching) The removal of socks from a human's washer or dryer is strictly prohibited. Separating pairs of socks—dress, casual, or other—will result in millions of households with mismatched socks. All illegal socks will be confiscated and turned over to the office of Naked Appendages.

How to Identify a Space Alien

A well-trained MIB agent should be able to recognize a space alien even when one is masquerading as a human. Below is a list of telltale signs that can help you identify aliens in human guise.

Claws: When retracted, claws—indigenous to both the cephlapoid and Arquillian species—look very much like human fingernails. Fully extended, these razor-sharp talons slice through human flesh like a knife through butter. The claws will involuntarily protrude from the ends of the fingers when the hands are fully spread.

Perspiration: Baltians, Slabobians, and Martians don't sweat. They pant like dogs. A home without deodorant in the medicine cabinet is indicative of alien activity. (It is also possible that the inhabitants are old hippies.)

Gills: Certain aliens—namely cephlapoids and Orkans—do not breathe oxygen. They filter air through gills hidden behind the eyelids. These gills are visible for a fraction of a second each time the creature blinks.

Feeding Habits: Space aliens love hot dogs. They are considered a delicacy in both the Zeldor and Omega Nine galaxies. Anyone seen eating hot dogs should be immediately suspected and detained for further questioning.

Allergies: Aliens, excluding Bugs, Oomish Kanish, and bipodic crustaceans, are allergic to chocolate. The enzyme necessary for cocoa digestion is missing. As a result, consumption of chocolate bars, cakes, cookies, or other baked goods can produce bloating, gastrointestinal discomfort, and vomiting. It may also cause uncontrollable drooling, convulsions, and a bright red body rash.

Skin: Sinaleans and Tuscolans molt twice a year on the eve of the winter and summer solstices. The new skin is smooth as a baby's butt. Later, the outer layer becomes crusty and callused, eventually taking on the feel and appearance of sandpaper. At certain times of the year, a firm handshake may be all that's necessary to justify an arrest. A word of caution: when the skin gets dry and cracks, it releases a putrid stench. If making an arrest, always approach suspect with moisturizer.

Mood Swings: Osmium-based life-forms are extremely sensitive to electromagnetic fields. Such extraterrestrials may suddenly become manic when exposed to high-tech hardware (i.e., racing around in circles, singing show tunes, and dancing the Macarena). Don't be fooled by creatures who refuse to enter particular establishments because they fear the microwave will set off their pacemakers. More likely, they are trying to avoid inducing a manic state, which might give away their true identity.

Fashion: Space aliens have real trouble catching on to earthly fashion trends. As a result, you should be on the lookout for beings dressed in particularly bad taste. Many aliens, for example, still think stonewashed jeans are in style. They have also been known to mix plaids and stripes and to carry combs in their back pockets.

Bizarre Sense of Humor: The emotions of extraterrestrials from the Zoltar Galaxy are wired to the opposite brain synapses as Earthlings. As a result, when a sad or painful event takes place, the alien laughs. Likewise, when a funny or enjoyable incident occurs, the alien cries. Beings observed laughing during funerals or crying at circuses should be brought down to MIB headquarters for immediate interrogation.

America's Most Wanted Aliens

CAPTURED

Name: EdgarBug

Human Alias: Edgar Smith
AKA: Lintboy, Boogler, Shmegley
Often Disguised As: Exterminator
Date of Birth: September 5, 1994
Race: Bugus giganticum
Sex: Male
Height: 12' 2"
Weight: 728 lbs.
Weakness: Raid Roach & Ant Killer
Crime: Galaxy-napping
Special note: This is the most vile creature in the universe.

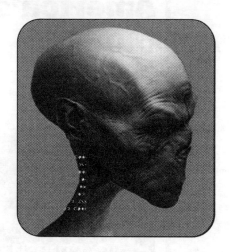

Name: Rolling Fish-Goat

Human Alias: Elmore Egghead

AKA: Pesci-Capra, Chuckles, Flipper

Often Disguised As: Guidance counselor

Date of Birth: January 24, 1812

Race: Zeta reticuli, capacious cranium anthropoid

Sex: 1/2 Male, 1/2 Female

Height: 3' 9"

Weight: 146 lbs.

Weakness: Anchovy pizza

Crime: Promulgating techno-rock

Special note: Prepares for combat by smacking itself on the head repeatedly.

Name: Bobo the Squat

Human Alias: Henry Marge Thomas

AKA: Gator, Mugsy, Vent-head

Often Disguised As: Disgruntled postal worker

Date of Birth: April 9, 600 B.C.

Race: Ytterbium

Sex: Unknown

Height: 3' 2"

Weight: 250 lbs.

Weakness: Extra dry skin; needs constant moisturizing

Crime: Conspiracy to expose true alien identity

Special note: Aggressive and destructive; an intergalactic bad seed.

Name: Elby-17

Human Alias: Harold Dweeble

AKA: Lobster Boy

Often Disguised As: Computer programmer with sweet tooth

Date of Birth: June 21, 2021 (time traveler)

Race: Bipodic crustacean

Sex: Male

Height: 5'11"

Weight: 160 lbs.

Weaknesses: Boiling water, melted butter

Crime: Massive chocolate theft

Special Note: Appears harmless, but looks can kill.

Name: Mitachon Dria

Human Alias: Bernadette Holdridge
AKA: Bubbles, Big Mama, Lady Lust
Often Disguised As: Massage therapist
Date of Birth: September 7, 1972
Race: Riggilian
Sex: Female
Height: 5'7" (5' 9" in heels)
Weight: 120 lbs.
Weaknesses: Men with dimples
Crime: Selling humans for alien experimentation

Special Note: Extremely dangerous. Invites men back to her apartment and then paralyzes them with a kiss.

Name: Yikem Xexaco

Human Alias: Jose Gonzales

AKA: Mikey

Often Disguised As: Migrant laborer

Date of Birth: June 21, 1496

Race: Samarium, amphibious bipedal form

Sex: Male

Height: 4' 6"

Weight: 160 lbs.

Weaknesses: Needs 10,000 calories a day to sustain life

Crime: Introduced alien artichoke species with nonremovable spines

Special Note: Violent and wildly unpredictable.

Name: Sleeble

Human Alias: Al Kelly

AKA: The Hacker

Date of Birth: August 3, 1979

Often Disguised As: Door-to-door encyclopedia salesman

Sex: Male

Height: 4' 2"

Weight: 580 lbs.

Weakness: Cheese-and-onion sandwiches

Crime: Spreading the Good Times computer virus

Special note: Communicates by making rude noises with his armpit.

Name: Ootrose Ootrose Ollie

Human Alias: Herbert Marmelstein

AKA: The Great Pretender

Often Disguised As: Chorus member from the Broadway musical *Cats*

Date of Birth: June 21, 1496

Race: Half human/half mergatroid

Sex: Male

Height: 5' 11"

Weight: 160 lbs.

Weaknesses: Left rear tentacle extremely ticklish

Crime: Space Piracy

Note: When agitated subject will expel jets of poisonous liquid from boils on face.

Name: Schliffler Van Schleeglotten

Human Alias: Skeeter Willaby

AKA: Tom, Dick, and Harry

Often Disguised As: Central Park hot-dog vendor

Date of Birth: 1954

Race: Oomish Kanish

Sex: Hermaphrodite

Height: 2' 11"

Weight: 30 lbs.

Weakness: Heavy winds

Crime: Sock Snatching

Taking a Suspect into Custody

Space aliens, like humans, are entitled to due process. If proper procedures are not followed, a guilty space alien could walk on a technicality. Therefore it is essential that agents adhere to the following procedures when taking a suspect into custody:

- Read suspect his/her Miranda rights.

- Once suspect has acknowledged that he/she understands his/her rights, he/she can be handcuffed. (Suspects without hands shall be cuffed around tentacles.)

- Drive suspect to headquarters for questioning.

* A criminal activity report (see page 31) must be filled out in triplicate and filed with Office of Alien Misconduct.

* Take alien's finger/tentacle prints.

* Take the alien's mug shot. Aliens of multiple form, be they animal, mineral, or vegetable, must be photographed in each of their various guises.

* Allow suspects to make one phone call before placing them in a holding cell. Calls within the 999 galaxy code will be paid for by the MIB. Aliens who wish to call outside the solar system must pay for the call with a credit card or reverse the charges.

Securing the Crime Scene

An MIB agent's role at the crime scene is twofold. First, make sure that the evidence is collected and recorded in a timely and orderly manner. Second, question any and all witnesses and then immediately erase their memory of the event. (See Permissible Use of a Neuralyzer, page 41.)

Only persons who have legitimate investigative interest should be allowed into a crime scene. Superfluous humans at a crime scene can lead to evidence being moved or destroyed before its value as evidence is recognized. Studies consistently show that too many cooks spoil the stew.

To ensure that important evidence is not overlooked, the following collection procedures should be routinely observed:

1. Photograph the crime scene before it has been disturbed.

2. Decide on a search pattern, i.e., lane, grid, spiral, or zone search.

3. Take special note of evidence that can be easily destroyed such as hoof prints in dust, slime deposits, and molted skin.

4. Cover up any trace of alien activity, e.g., remove dead aliens or body parts.

5. Call for a Containment Unit if backup is needed, or for pick-up of abandoned spacecraft.

MEN IN BLACK
CRIMINAL ACTIVITY REPORT

Suspect's name Mikey

Address 911 Elm Street   **Planet** Samaria

Solar System Omega 19   **Galaxy** I/T

Eye color _____   **Fur color** (if applicable) _____

Antennae Y ☑ N ☐   **Height** 4' 6" **Weight** 85

Other distinguishing marks Tattoo on left shoulder
blade, "Aliens Make Better Coffee"

Nature of crime: Introduced alien artichoke species
with nonremovable spines

This is a violation of:
☑ State law ☑ Universal law ☐ Newton's law

☑ Federal law ☑ Interplanetary law

☐ Murphy's law

Location of crime: Rural area near Brownsville, Texas
(If place of business, state name and address of establishment)

Crime occured ⊙n /between this day/date 5/26/97
and _____
Was a vehicle involved in this crime? Y ☑ N ☐
(If Yes, answer the following:)

Vehicle type:
☐ UFO   ☐ Rocket   ☐ Sport Utility Vehicle

☐ Car ☑ Van Color _____ Year 89

Make _____ Model _____

☑ Stored/impounded

Narrative: In your own words, describe the facts
surrounding the arrest:
Suspect was posing as one of a group of Mexican
immigrants when approached by MIB Agents. When
suspect failed to respond to questions asked of him
in Spanish, Agent Kay took him into custody. Subject
attempted to flee and as a result he was vaporized
into a geyser of blue goo.

Transportation

The MIB has a fleet of 12 specially equipped Ford LTDs for use by agents on street beats. All cars are parked in the agency parking structure. Take the elevators to sub-level five. Keys are to be left in the ignition. You may bring your parking stub to the fourth floor reception desk for validation.

Cars should be fueled with certified rocket fuel only.

All vehicles are equipped with an AM/FM stereo, air-conditioning, power steering, power windows and locks, and a few additional features outlined below.

Floatable tires: When submerged in more than two feet of water, tires will hyperinflate, making car buoyant.

Multiple-use headlights: For urban night driving, leave the headlights on low beam. On lightly traveled roads, switch the headlights to high beam for better illumination. On roads besieged by alien aggressors, switch to super-high beam. The 100,000-watt bulbs are designed to temporarily blind your assailants.

Fast Forward: To defy gravity and travel at speeds in excess of 400 miles per hour, press the red button on the console between the two front seats.

Funny Fumes: To expel laughing gas from the exhaust pipe, move the gear shift into Drive Three. Any and all aliens within a 30-foot radius of the car will be immobilized by an uncontrollable fit of laughter. (Sinaleans seem not to be affected, as they have no sense of humor.)

Bulletproof Windshield: The windows of the LTDs are impervious to bullets. However, agents are advised to drive slowly on gravel roads as fast-moving pebbles may cause the glass to crack.

✳ PLEASE NOTE: LTDS ARE FOR OFFICIAL USE ONLY. ANY AGENT CAUGHT JOYRIDING WILL BE IMMEDIATELY TERMINATED.

TRAVEL

The MIB has set up a corporate account with the interplanetary travel agency Nebulas Travel. Should your assignment require you to leave Earth, contact Nebulas Travel as soon as possible to ensure that we can get the best possible fare.

All MIB agents must travel coach class, unless your travel plans take you to another dimension. Fourth and fifth dimension travelers may fly business class. Seventh dimension travelers are permitted to fly first class but only when taking the red-eye. Beings with perpetually red eyes must fly business class.

✳ Frequent flier miles accrued while on assignment become the property of the MIB.

Alien Vessels—Humans often dismiss alien spacecraft as weather balloons, blimps, or high-tech military planes. As an MIB agent, you must be able to tell the difference. Familiarize yourself with the following photos and technology descriptions. This information will be crucial should you ever need to commandeer an alien spacecraft. Descriptions accompanied by photos.

LYRAN CRUISER

Engine: Uses a basic antigraviton generator for interplanetary travel and an Okuda "M" type power thruster for interdimensional treks. Once safely outside the Solar System, the intersteller booster can be used to propel the ship to maximum fourth dimension speed.

Artillery: Two forward-firing laser cannons

Maximum Speed: 12 light-years per hour

Passenger Capacity: 400 beings

Fuel Type: Flatulence

Miles per gallon: 200,000,000,000,000,000,000

Safety Features: Five self-propellant escape pods, driver-side airbag, and antilock brakes

Purpose: Civilian intergalactic transport

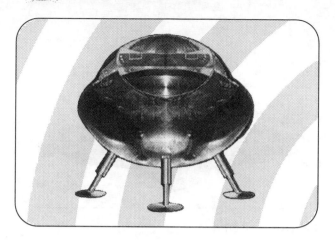

Venusian Taxi

Engine: Powered by six Sinalean B-9 ion engines. Should the ion engines fail, the vessel will automatically switch to a twin-engine propeller system.

Artillery: The pilot carries a gun

Maximum Speed: The Venusian Taxi travels at a modest speed of only 100,000 kilometers an hour.

Passenger Capacity: 5 beings

Fuel Type: Runs best on plutonium, but diesel can be substituted in a pinch

Miles per gallon: 900,000,000

Safety Features: Driver-side airbag and child safety locks.

Purpose: Shuttles passengers from the dark side of the moon to a floating landing strip 180 miles due east of New York harbor.

ANDROMEDIAN CRUISER

Engine: Quadrex water-cooled fluoron engine with two individually adjustable power thrust nozzles.*

Artillery: Front and rear laser cannons

Maximum Speed: Faster than you can say, "Let's bag some bug."

Passenger Capacity: 4 beings (50 Inka Dinkas)

Fuel Type: Tabasco sauce

Miles per per gallon: 112,000,000,000

Safety Features: Traction control, driver- and passenger-side airbags and roll bar (convertible version only)

Purpose: Seek out new life forms. Go where no man has gone before. Wait, no that's another show. This is a cargo ship.

* This model is sold with a standard five-speed shifter, but can be special ordered in automatic.

ZETA BEAMSHIP

Engine: Rear-mount magna SRT-lift engine with hyper-drive capabilities.

Artillery: Four heat-seeking proton torpedoes, three atomic bombs, two laser cannons, and a partridge in a pear tree.

Maximum Speed: Lickity Split

Passenger Capacity: 1,000 beings

Fuel Type: Nitroglycerin

Miles Per Gallon: 30,000 (40,000 on the skyway)

Safety Features: Asteroid deflector panels, antilock brakes

Purpose: Military reconnaissance

Weapons Catalog

On-duty MIB agents must be armed and ready for battle. Firearms should be employed if an agent feels his life or a fellow human being's life is in immediate jeopardy.

All agents will be assigned a firearm. (For a description of MIB-approved weaponry, see below). Agents who opt to use the Series 4 De-Atomizer must first report for a mandatory six-week training course. Use by untrained marksmen is strictly prohibited.

A **carbonizer with implosion capacity** discharges an alien gas called carbon X-11. It has a fogging radius of 100 feet. Fumes are so toxic they can vaporize human flesh in 12 seconds. (Available in midnight black and spaceman silver).

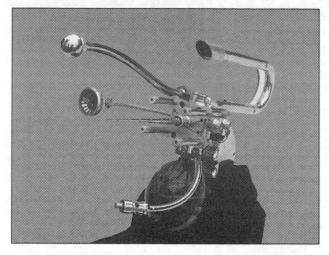

CARBONIZER WITH IMPLOSION CAPACITY

The **Noisy Cricket** may look harmless, but this lightweight 12-shot hand gun is incredibly powerful. The hairpin trigger releases a + p + 110-Grain JHP bullet with 8,932 fps velocity.

The **Series 4 De-Atomizer** is a triple-barreled shotgun, with a pump action reloader and a built-in storage clip for 12 additional shells. The rifle can be adjusted to one of the following five settings.

Level 1: Squirt Gun

Level 2: Sling Shot

Level 3: BB Gun

Level 4: Bazooka

Level 5: Atomic machine gun

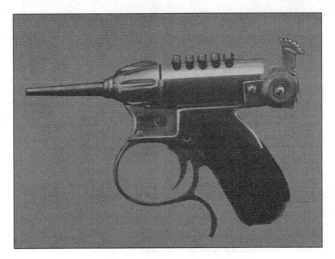

THE NOISY CRICKET

Permissible Use of a Neuralyzer

The neuralyzer is an indispensable tool. This instrument emits laser light that can penetrate the human skull and block memory impulses to the brain. If a human accidentally witnesses alien activity, the neuralyzer may be used to erase that memory.

The neuralyzer should not be employed indiscriminately. Agents must decide on a case-by-case basis who and when to neuralyze. If the person witnessing the alien encounter lacks credibility, or if the sighting can somehow be dismissed as a nonalien paranormal phenomenon (ghost, goblin, or poltergeist), refrain from firing. As a rule, citizens of towns with populations under 150 are not considered credible witnesses.

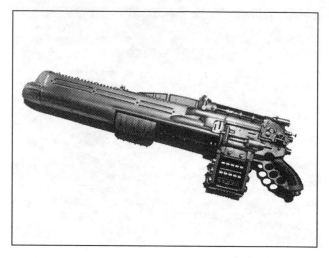

THE SERIES 4 DE-ATOMIZER

Agents are required to fill out an incident report form each time they activate the neuralyzer. The report should include time and date of the incident, as well as a detailed description of the lost memory.

Use of a neuralyzer for anything other than official MIB business is a federal offense punishable by up to 50 years in orbit.

Special authorization: Agents who have left behind family and friends are allotted free use of the neuralyzer to attend family and high school reunions.

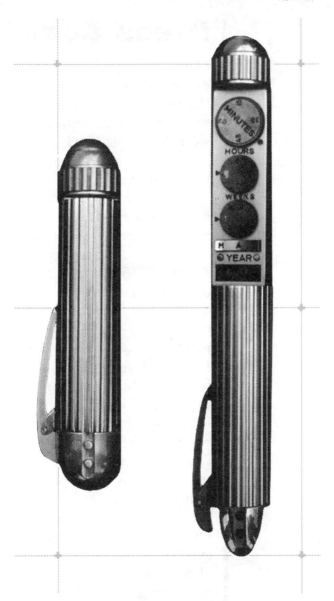

NEURALYZERS

Dress Code

MIB agents are impeccably dressed. The uniform should consist of all of the following: black suit, white shirt, black tie, black socks, black shoes, and black sunglasses.

From September through March, suits must be made of worsted wool or wool gabardine. From April until August, cotton or linen. Men in Black do not wear polyester. It's not only ugly, it's highly flammable.

Official underwear style for the MIB is boxers, not briefs. Our apologies to former brief wearers for any inconvenience this may cause. Compliance with this dictum is based on the honor system.

Shoe style is the one area where agents are encouraged to express individuality. You may wear black loafers with or without tassels.

Agents receive a clothing allowance of $10,000 a year. This money can be spent only at MIB-approved stores (see your supervisor).

General Appearance: MIB employees must be adequately dressed for duty. Uniform garments should be properly fitted and maintained in a clean, neat, and serviceable condition. First impressions are important. Men in Black are Earth's ambassadors and as such are expected to represent the human race in the best possible light.

Laundry: Suits should never be worn more than once without being dry-cleaned. Shirts should be laundered using light to medium starch. A company-issue lint brush can be obtained at the MIB's Sanitation Department.

Hair: Hair should be kept neat and in a style that's simple and inconspicuous. No restrictions are placed on length, but George Clooney cuts are strongly discouraged. Mohawks, dreadlocks, and Jennifer Anistons are strictly prohibited.

Shaving: MIB employees are required to shave daily. Agents with particularly sensitive skin must ask their dermatologists to fill out a daily shaving waiver form. Agents who wish to grow a beard or mustache should first seek approval from their supervisor. Sideburns and goatees will not be tolerated. Men in Black set trends. We do not follow them.

The Immigration Center

Identity Cards

All aliens are required to register with the Immigration Center upon arrival. First-time visitors must stop by the identity desk to be fitted with a humanoid body and to receive their resident alien cards (see the next page). Return visitors can proceed immediately to customs.

Special Note: Many aliens request the assumed identity of Elvis Presley. Agents may honor this petition, but restrict subjects' travel to the greater Las Vegas area.

Visas

Visas must be obtained at least six weeks prior to arrival. No exceptions. Aliens may apply for a three-week, three-month, or three-year stay. A background check on each applicant must be completed before a visa is issued. If the investigation turns up evidence that the applicant has been convicted of assault, battery, or copyright infringement, access to the planet shall be denied.

Travel Restrictions

Only visitors with MFA (Most Favored Alien) status can wander the planet freely. The vast majority of aliens shall be restricted to the five boroughs of New York. Requests for alternate destinations will be reviewed on a case-by-case basis. Place a restricted travel stamp on the

alien's passport indicating specific latitudinal and longitudinal boundaries. Should an alien need to leave the restricted area, said alien can return to the Immigration Center and apply for a transcontinental day pass.

Customs

MIB agents have the right to perform a strip search and inspect the body cavities of all suspicious-looking visitors. (Suspect activities include carrying: large quantities of cash, weapons of mass destruction, or vials of virulent bacteria.) Any alien that refuses to be searched shall be immediately deported. Aliens are forbidden from bringing in foreign fruits or vegetables, unless cleared with Agricultural Affairs prior to landing.

Unauthorized produce will be confiscated and eaten.

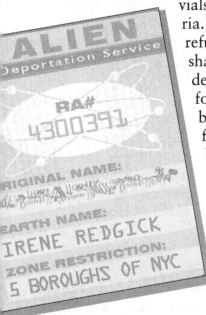

Illegal Aliens

The gaping whole in the Earth's ozone layer has become the source of a steady stream of illegal aliens. Each year, hundreds penetrate the atmosphere and land their spacecraft without official clearance. Most of these extraterrestrials are hard-working aliens hoping to escape space poverty and forge a better life. But a few are sinister creatures from far away galaxies who want nothing more than to rape and pillage the Earth and its resources.

An MIB agent who encounters an undocumented alien shall take the being into custody immediately. Upon arrival at MIB headquarters, space beings are to be escorted directly to the office of WHAT ON EARTH ARE YOU DOING HERE? for a thorough interrogation.

If the interrogation turns up evidence of alien misconduct, the suspect will be detained until such time as his or her criminal actions can be determined by an intergalactic tribunal. If found guilty, the suspect will be brought back for sentencing.

Asylum

Illegal aliens found innocent of criminal wrongdoing will be deported on the next comet out of town. However, if said alien has valid reasons for seeking asylum, said alien can fill out a petition for asylum (see page 52). An agent from the office of WHAT ON EARTH ARE YOU DOING

HERE? will review this request and said alien will receive a response within five working eons. Until such time, said alien shall remain in the custody of the MIB.

IMMIGRATION

PETITION FOR ASYLUM

Applicant's Name Nilto Tralfaz Solarberg

                            First   Middle   Last

Address 110 Hale-Bopp Way

Solar System Alpha Reculi **Galaxy** Zeldor

Please indicate the type of asylum you are applying for:

☐ political   ☑ metaphysical

☐ transcendental   ☐ religious

☐ sane   ☐ soul

Do you have any relatives living on earth?

Mavis 12 (third cousin twice removed)

(if yes, please specify the nature of your relationship.)

If you were to be granted asylum, what innovation or technology could you bring us?

Telepathically activated TV remote

What is your present level of education:

☐ grammar school ☐ middle school

☐ high school   ☐ space academy

☑ Beta school of combat ☐ college

In addition to your native tongue, do you speak (circle where applicable):

☐ Swahili   ☑ English   ☐ French

☐ binary   ☑ Martian   ☑ Pig Latin

☐ Spanish   ☐ Pennsylvania Dutch

☐ hieroglyphic   ☑ Sinalean

Narrative: In your own words, tell us why you plan to immigrate to this planet legally.

Ever since I was a little Hebble Jebble I've been told that Earth was the land of opportunity, a place where if you worked hard and paid your dues you could be whatever you wanted to be and do whatever you wanted to do. My dream is to open a chain of luxury hotels for cats and dogs.

Headquarters Office Protocols

Arrival and Departure

Concealing the whereabouts of the MIB headquarters is a matter of intergalactic security. Agents are to exercise extreme caution when entering or exiting the building. When departing, keep your head down, and merge with the sidewalk traffic. When returning to headquarters, it is imperative that agents refrain from singing "I'm a Yankee Doodle Dandy" at the top of your lungs, as this tends to attract unnecessary attention.

Intergalactic Dating

If an MIB agent should decide to pursue a relationship with an otherworldly being, the policy is as follows: Don't ask, don't tell. The agency neither condones nor condemns intergalactic marriages. But be forewarned: Should an agent have a child with an alien of any species, intergalactic law mandates that sole custody of the offspring be given to the being of higher intelligence. (The only beings less intelligent than humans are space slugs and asteroid mites.)

Work Hours

MIB agents work on Centaurian time (a 37-hour day). Of that day, agents are on duty 16 hours. If it is necessary for you to work overtime, you will be paid for additional service at a rate of one and a half times your hourly rate. Vacation days can be taken once in a blue moon.

The following holidays are observed by the MIB.

New Year's Day, January 1
Martin Luther King's Birthday, the second Monday in January
Intergalactic Unity Day, February 10
Memorial Day, the last Monday in May
Extraterrestrial Appreciation Day, June 24
Independence Day, July 4
Yom Kippur, the 10th day of Tishri
Christmas, December 25

Expense Reports

An expense report must be completed within 10 days after an MIB agent incurs expenses on behalf of the agency. Below are examples of reimbursable expenses:

> oxygen tanks
>
> moon suits
>
> dry-cleaning for slimed outerwear
>
> meals with intergalactic dignitaries
>
> tabloid newspapers
>
> fake mustaches, beards, and tentacles
>
> calls outside the 999 galaxy code
>
> antigravity shoes

Please use one expense report per assignment and indicate the job number for all appropriate expenses associated with that assignment. (See the next page for sample expense report form.)

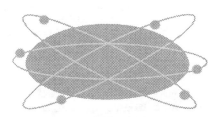

MEN IN BLACK ™

Employee Name: Bee

Date: 6/30/97

Billable Expense Report

Date	Reimbursable Item	Purpose of Expense	Money Was Paid to:	Bill to Job #
6/21	dry-cleaning bill	remove goo from suit lapel	The Lucky Shirt 911 W 6th St. NY, NY Planet Earth	86753
6/22	Martian costume	undercover assignment	Boo! I Scared You Novelty Store 12 Orchard St. NY, NY Planet Earth	7773
6/23	Hotel Room	moderated discussions at the Baltian Arquillian peace talks	Celestial Inn and Convention Center 209 Cosmic Way Iko Ikko, Gryso Planet XOXO	3834
6/24	dinner	meet and greet for the deposed sur-prefect of Sinalee	Cowboy Bob's Steak House 334 Ash Street Portland, Oregon	2482

Total Expense: _____ $282.16 _____

Less Cash Advance Balance:_____ $182.16 _____

Employee Signature: Bee _____

Insurance

The MIB provides full medical and dental insurance coverage to become effective 30 days after employment. When you sign up for this program, you must choose a primary care physician from our list of health-care providers. Our directory contains names of doctors throughout the galaxy. So should you become ill, injured, or frozen into a state of suspended animation while working on another planet, your medical expenses will be covered. There is no deductible, and hospital services are covered 100% except for the emergency room co-pay of $25.

401(k)

You may contribute up to 13% of your pay, on a before-tax basis, up to the maximum allowed by the

IRS each year. MIB will match 50 cents for every $1 you contribute up to a maximum of 13% of your salary. You may direct your 401(k) savings to any or all of the following investment categories:

* Intergalactic Funds
* Aggressive Growth Funds
* Arquillian War Bonds
* Baltian Treasury Bills

Termination/Severance

From time to time, it is necessary for employees to leave their jobs. This can be voluntary (personal reasons) or involuntary (you stink at your job). Before you can end your employment, you must return all MIB property, including identification cards, secret decoder rings, and the key to the executive washroom.

If you are involuntarily separated (fired because you did a lousy job), you are still eligible for two weeks of severance pay plus one additional week for each year of service thereafter. Career counseling is also available for displaced agents.

* *Special Note: Just because you made a lousy agent doesn't mean you can't go on to enjoy a rich and fulfilling career as a mall security guard.*

Discrimination and Sexual Harassment

The MIB will conduct its affairs free from unlawful discrimination and sexual harassment. It provides equal opportunity and treatment for all members irrespective of their race, fur color, religion, intergalactic origin, sex, age, or ability to breathe fluorocarbons.

Whenever unlawful discrimination is found, the MIB will make every effort to eliminate it and neutralize the effects. Supervisors who are aware of unlawful discrimination by subordinates but fail to take action will be disciplined (i.e., no TV, car, or phone privileges for a month).

Any of the following elements may constitute sexual harassment or discrimination:

Physical Contact: Squeezing a worker's shoulder or putting a hand around his or her waist, fondling a tail, or caressing an antenna.

Gestures: Puckering one's lips suggestively or making obscene signs with one's finger or tentacle.

Jokes: Telling off-color, ethnic, or racial jokes. (Example: How many Klingons does it take to change a lightbulb? Two, one to screw in the bulb and another to shoot him and take the credit.)

Pictures: Pinups, particularly those of scantily clad extraterrestrials.

Comments: Generalities that lump one group together and denigrate them. (Example: Oomish Kanish are all a bunch of crooks and liars.)

Terms of Endearment Calling a coworker "honey," "dear," "sucker lips," or some similar expression. The effect is the primary issue rather than intent. Even if the being means nothing to you or you have used the term for years, you should be aware that these expressions are inappropriate.

Questionable Compliments: "Nice legs!" or "Wow, you look hot in those anti-gravity boots!" Compliments like these can make individuals feel uncomfortable.

In Case of Alien Invasion

Please cut out the following alien attack procedure notice and post it in a prominent position somewhere in your work space.

1. Remain calm.

2. Alert others on your floor.

3. Disseminate this information in a composed and relaxed manner. Here is a sample script of what you might say to avoid panic among your coworkers. "Hi, this is (fill in your name), and we're about to get blasted by a fleet of Arquillian Battle Cruisers wielding high-velocity laser cannons. So I suggest we all make like sheepherders and get the flock out of here!"

4. Move away from windows, glass, and outside doors and walls.

5. Get under a desk or table and cover your head.

6. Stay inside. Falling debris and radioactive fallout poses a serious threat. You are safer inside the building than out.

7. If taken captive by extraterrestrials, tell them nothing other than your name, rank, and serial number.

WARNING!

The contents of this manual
are fully protected under
intergalatic copyright law.

UNAUTHORIZED
USERS WILL BE
NEURALYZED!

CLASSIFIED